The Sisters

(Volume 4)

Georg Ebers

Alpha Editions

This edition published in 2023

ISBN : 9789357958974

Design and Setting By
Alpha Editions
www.alphaedis.com
Email - info@alphaedis.com

Contents

CHAPTER XVII...- 1 -

CHAPTER XVIII..- 6 -

CHAPTER XIX. ....- 17 -

CHAPTER XX...- 30 -

CHAPTER XXI. ....- 38 -

CHAPTER XVII.

A paved road, with a row of Sphinxes on each side, led from the Greek temple of Serapis to the rock-hewn tombs of Apis, and the temples and chapels built over them, and near them; in these the Apis bull after its death—or "in Osiris" as the phrase went—was worshipped, while, so long as it lived, it was taken care of and prayed to in the temple to which it belonged, that of the god Ptah at Memphis. After death these sacred bulls, which were distinguished by peculiar marks, had extraordinarily costly obsequies; they were called the risen Ptah, and regarded as the symbol of the soul of Osiris, by whose procreative power all that dies or passes away is brought to new birth and new life—the departed soul of man, the plant that has perished, and the heavenly bodies that have set. Osiris-Sokari, who was worshipped as the companion of Osiris, presided over the wanderings which had to be performed by the seemingly extinct spirit before its resuscitation as another being in a new form; and Egyptian priests governed in the temples of these gods, which were purely Egyptian in style, and which had been built at a very early date over the tomb-cave of the sacred bulls. And even the Greek ministers of Serapis, settled at Memphis, were ready to follow the example of their rulers and to sacrifice to Osiris-Apis, who was closely allied to Serapis—not only in name but in his essential attributes. Serapis himself indeed was a divinity introduced from Asia into the Nile valley by the Ptolemies, in order to supply to their Greek and Egyptian subjects alike an object of adoration, before whose altars they could unite in a common worship. They devoted themselves to the worship of Apis in Osiris at the shrines, of Greek architecture, and containing stone images of bulls, that stood outside the Egyptian sanctuary, and they were very ready to be initiated into the higher significance of his essence; indeed, all religious mysteries in their Greek home bore reference to the immortality of the soul and its fate in the other world.

Just as two neighboring cities may be joined by a bridge, so the Greek temple of Serapis—to which the water-bearers belonged—was connected with the Egyptian sanctuary of Osiris-Apis by the fine paved road for processions along which Klea now rapidly proceeded. There was a shorter way to Memphis, but she chose this one, because the mounds of sand on each side of the road bordered by Sphinxes—which every day had to be cleared of the desert-drift—concealed her from the sight of her companions in the temple; besides the best and safest way into the city was by a road leading from a crescent, decorated with busts of the philosophers, that lay near the principal entrance to the new Apis tombs.

She looked neither at the lion-bodies with men's heads that guarded the way, nor at the images of beasts on the wall that shut it in; nor did she heed the dusky-hued temple-slaves of Osiris-Apis who were sweeping the sand from the paved way with large brooms, for she thought of nothing but Irene and the difficult task that lay before her, and she walked swiftly onwards with her eyes fixed on the ground.

But she had taken no more than a few steps when she heard her name called quite close to her, and looking up in alarm she found herself standing opposite Krates, the little smith, who came close up to her, took hold of her veil, threw it back a little before she could prevent him, and asked:

"Where are you off to, child?"

"Do not detain me," entreated Klea. "You know that Irene, whom you are always so fond of, has been carried off; perhaps I may be able to save her, but if you betray me, and if they follow me—"

"I will not hinder you," interrupted the old man. "Nay, if it were not for these swollen feet I would go with you, for I can think of nothing else but the poor dear little thing; but as it is I shall be glad enough when I am sitting still again in my workshop; it is exactly as if a workman of my own trade lived in each of my great toes, and was dancing round in them with hammer and file and chisel and nails. Very likely you may be so fortunate as to find your sister, for a crafty woman succeeds in many things which are too difficult for a wise man. Go on, and if they seek for you old Krates will not betray you."

He nodded kindly at Klea, and had already half turned his back on her when he once more looked round, and called out to her:

"Wait a minute, girl—you can do me a little service. I have just fitted a new lock to the door of the Apis-tomb down there. It answers admirably, but the one key to it which I have made is not enough; we require four, and you shall order them for me of the locksmith Heri, to be sent the day after to-morrow; he lives opposite the gate of Sokari— to the left, next the bridge over the canal—you cannot miss it. I hate repeating and copying as much as I like inventing and making new things, and Heri can work from a pattern just as well as I can. If it were not for my legs I would give the man my commission myself, for he who speaks by the lips of a go-between is often misunderstood or not understood at all."

"I will gladly save you the walk," replied Klea, while the Smith sat down on the pedestal of one of the Sphinxes, and opening the leather wallet which hung by his side shook out the contents. A few files, chisels, and nails fell out into his lap; then the key, and finally a sharp, pointed knife with which Krates had cut out the hollow in the door for the insertion of the lock;

Krates touched up the pattern-key for the smith in Memphis with a few strokes of the file, and then, muttering thoughtfully and shaking his head doubtfully from side to side, he exclaimed:

"You still must come with me once more to the door, for I require accurate workmanship from other people, and so I must be severe upon my own."

"But I want so much to reach Memphis before dark," besought Klea.

"The whole thing will not take a minute, and if you will give me your arm I shall go twice as fast. There are the files, there is the knife."

"Give it me," Klea requested. "This blade is sharp and bright, and as soon as I saw it I felt as if it bid me take it with me. Very likely I may have to come through the desert alone at night."

"Aye," said the smith, "and even the weakest feels stronger when he has a weapon. Hide the knife somewhere about you, my child, only take care not to hurt yourself with it. Now let me take your arm, and on we will go— but not quite so fast."

Klea led the smith to the door he indicated, and saw with admiration how unfailingly the bolt sprang forward when one half of the door closed upon the other, and how easily the key pushed it back again; then, after conducting Krates back to the Sphinx near which she had met him, she went on her way at her quickest pace, for the sun was already very low, and it seemed scarcely possible to reach Memphis before it should set.

As she approached a tavern where soldiers and low people were accustomed to resort, she was met by a drunken slave. She went on and past him without any fear, for the knife in her girdle, and on which she kept her hand, kept up her courage, and she felt as if she had thus acquired a third hand which was more powerful and less timid than her own. A company of soldiers had encamped in front of the tavern, and the wine of Kbakem, which was grown close by, on the eastern declivity of the Libyan range, had an excellent savor. The men were in capital spirits, for at noon today—after they had been quartered here for months as guards of the tombs of Apis and of the temples of the Necropolis—a commanding officer of the Diadoches had arrived at Memphis, who had ordered them to break up at once, and to withdraw into the capital before nightfall. They were not to be relieved by other mercenaries till the next morning.

All this Klea learned from a messenger from the Egyptian temple in the Necropolis, who recognized her, and who was going to Memphis, commissioned by the priests of Osiris-Apis and Sokari to convey a petition to the king, praying that fresh troops might be promptly sent to replace those now withdrawn.

For some time she went on side by side with this messenger, but soon she found that she could not keep up with his hurried pace, and had to fall behind. In front of another tavern sat the officers of the troops, whose noisy mirth she had heard as she passed the former one; they were sitting over their wine and looking on at the dancing of two Egyptian girls, who screeched like cackling hens over their mad leaps, and who so effectually riveted the attention of the spectators, who were beating time for them by clapping their hands, that Klea, accelerating her step, was able to slip unobserved past the wild crew. All these scenes, nay everything she met with on the high-road, scared the girl who was accustomed to the silence and the solemn life of the temple of Serapis, and she therefore struck into a side path that probably also led to the city which she could already see lying before her with its pylons, its citadel and its houses, veiled in evening mist. In a quarter of an hour at most she would have crossed the desert, and reach the fertile meadow land, whose emerald hue grew darker and darker every moment. The sun was already sinking to rest behind the Libyan range, and soon after, for twilight is short in Egypt, she was wrapped in the darkness of night. The westwind, which had begun to blow even at noon, now rose higher, and seemed to pursue her with its hot breath and the clouds of sand it carried with it from the desert.

She must certainly be approaching water, for she heard the deep pipe of the bittern in the reeds, and fancied she breathed a moister air. A few steps more, and her foot sank in mud; and she now perceived that she was standing on the edge of a wide ditch in which tall papyrus-plants were growing. The side path she had struck into ended at this plantation, and there was nothing to be done but to turn about, and to continue her walk against the wind and with the sand blowing in her face.

The light from the drinking-booth showed her the direction she must follow, for though the moon was up, it is true, black clouds swept across it, covering it and the smaller lights of heaven for many minutes at a time. Still she felt no fatigue, but the shouts of the men and the loud cries of the women that rang out from the tavern filled her with alarm and disgust. She made a wide circuit round the hostelry, wading through the sand hillocks and tearing her dress on the thorns and thistles that had boldly struck deep root in the desert, and had grown up there like the squalid brats in the hovel of a beggar. But still, as she hurried on by the high-road, the hideous laughter and the crowing mirth of the dancing-girls still rang in her mind's ear.

Her blood coursed more swiftly through her veins, her head was on fire, she saw Irene close before her, tangibly distinct—with flowing hair and fluttering garments, whirling in a wild dance like a Moenad at a Dionysiac festival, flying from one embrace to another and shouting and shrieking in unbridled folly like the wretched girls she had seen on her way. She was seized with terror for her sister—an unbounded dread such as she had never felt before, and as the wind was now once more behind her she let herself be driven on by it, lifting her feet in a swift run and flying, as if pursued by the Erinnyes, without once looking round her and wholly forgetful of the smith's commission, on towards the city along the road planted with trees, which as she knew led to the gate of the citadel.

CHAPTER XVIII.

In front of the gate of the king's palace sat a crowd of petitioners who were accustomed to stay here from early dawn till late at night, until they were called into the palace to receive the answer to the petition they had drawn up. When Klea reached the end of her journey she was so exhausted and bewildered that she felt the imperative necessity of seeking rest and quiet reflection, so she seated herself among these people, next to a woman from Upper Egypt. But hardly had she taken her place by her with a silent greeting, when her talkative neighbor began to relate with particular minuteness why she had come to Memphis, and how certain unjust judges had conspired with her bad husband to trick her— for men were always ready to join against a woman—and to deprive her of everything which had been secured to her and her children by her marriage-contract. For two months now, she said, she had been waiting early and late before the sublime gate, and was consuming her last ready cash in the city where living was so dear; but it was all one to her, and at a pinch she would sell even her gold ornaments, for sooner or later her cause must come before the king, and then the wicked villain and his accomplices would be taught what was just.

Klea heard but little of this harangue; a feeling had come over her like that of a person who is having water poured again and again on the top of his head. Presently her neighbor observed that the new-comer was not listening at all to her complainings; she slapped her shoulder with her hand, and said:

"You seem to think of nothing but your own concerns; and I dare say they are not of such a nature as that you should relate them to any one else; so far as mine are concerned the more they are discussed, the better."

The tone in which these remarks were made was so dry, and at the same time so sharp, that it hurt Klea, and she rose hastily to go closer to the gate. Her neighbor threw a cross word after her; but she did not heed it, and drawing her veil closer over her face, she went through the gate of the palace into a vast courtyard, brightly lighted up by cressets and torches, and crowded with foot-soldiers and mounted guards.

The sentry at the gate perhaps had not observed her, or perhaps had let her pass unchallenged from her dignified and erect gait, and the numerous armed men through whom she now made her way seemed to be so much occupied with their own affairs, that no one bestowed any notice on her. In a narrow alley, which led to a second court and was lighted by lanterns, one of the body-guard known as Philobasilistes, a haughty young fellow in yellow riding-boots and a shirt of mail over his red tunic, came riding towards her on his tall horse, and noticing her he tried to squeeze her between his charger and the wall, and put out his hand to raise her veil; but Klea slipped aside, and put up her hands to protect herself from the horse's head which was almost touching her.

The cavalier, enjoying her alarm, called out: "Only stand still—he is not vicious."

"Which, you or your horse?" asked Klea, with such a solemn tone in her deep voice that for an instant the young guardsman lost his self- possession, and this gave her time to go farther from the horse. But the girl's sharp retort had annoyed the conceited young fellow, and not having time to follow her himself, he called out in a tone of encouragement to a party of mercenaries from Cyprus, whom the frightened girl was trying to pass:

"Look under this girl's veil, comrades, and if she is as pretty as she is well-grown, I wish you joy of your prize." He laughed as he pressed his knees against the flanks of his bay and trotted slowly away, while the Cypriotes gave Klea ample time to reach the second court, which was more brightly lighted even than the first, that they might there surround her with insolent importunity.

The helpless and persecuted girl felt the blood run cold in her veins, and for a few minutes she could see nothing but a bewildering confusion of flashing eyes and weapons, of beards and hands, could hear nothing but words and sounds, of which she understood and felt only that they were revolting and horrible, and threatened her with death and ruin. She had crossed her arms over her bosom, but now she raised her hands to hide her face, for she felt a strong hand snatch away the veil that covered her head. This insolent proceeding turned her numb horror to indignant rage, and, fixing her sparkling eyes on her bearded opponents, she exclaimed:

"Shame upon you, who in the king's own house fall like wolves on a defenceless woman, and in a peaceful spot snatch the veil from a young girl's head. Your mothers would blush for you, and your sisters cry shame on you—as I do now!"

Astonished at Klea's distinguished beauty, startled at the angry glare in her eyes, and the deep chest-tones of her voice which trembled with excitement, the Cypriotes drew back, while the same audacious rascal that had pulled away her veil came closer to her, and cried:

"Who would make such a noise about a rubbishy veil! If you will be my sweetheart I will buy you a new one, and many things besides."

At the same time he tried to throw his arm round her; but at his touch Klea felt the blood leave her cheeks and mount to her bloodshot eyes, and at that instant her hand, guided by some uncontrollable inward impulse, grasped the handle of the knife which Krates had lent her; she raised it high in the air though with an unsteady arm, exclaiming:

"Let me go or, by Serapis whom I serve, I will strike you to the heart!"

The soldier to whom this threat was addressed, was not the man to be intimidated by a blade of cold iron in a woman's hand; with a quick movement he seized her wrist in order to disarm her; but although Klea was forced to drop the knife she struggled with him to free herself from his clutch, and this contest between a man and a woman, who seemed to be of superior rank to that indicated by her very simple dress, seemed to most of the Cypriotes so undignified, so much out of place within the walls of a palace, that they pulled their comrade back from Klea, while others on the contrary came to the assistance of the bully who defended himself stoutly. And in the midst of the fray, which was conducted with no small noise, stood Klea with flying breath. Her antagonist, though flung to the ground, still held her wrist with his left hand while he defended himself against his comrades with the right, and she tried with all her force and cunning to withdraw it; for at the very height of her excitement and danger she felt as if a sudden gust of wind had swept her spirit clear of all confusion, and she was again able to contemplate her position calmly and resolutely.

If only her hand were free she might perhaps be able to take advantage of the struggle between her foes, and to force her way out between their ranks.

Twice, thrice, four times, she tried to wrench her hand with a sudden jerk through the fingers that grasped it; but each time in vain. Suddenly, from the man at her feet there broke a loud, long-drawn cry of pain which re-echoed from the high walls of the court, and at the same time she felt the fingers of her antagonist gradually and slowly slip from her arm like the straps of a sandal carefully lifted by the surgeon from a broken ankle.

"It is all over with him!" exclaimed the eldest of the Cypriotes. "A man never calls out like that but once in his life! True enough—the dagger is sticking here just under the ninth rib! This is mad work! That is your doing again, Lykos, you savage wolf!"

"He bit deep into my finger in the struggle—"

"And you are for ever tearing each other to pieces for the sake of the women," interrupted the elder, not listening to the other's excuses. "Well, I was no better than you in my time, and nothing can alter it! You had better be off now, for if the Epistrategist learns we have fallen to stabbing each other again—"

The Cypriote had not ceased speaking, and his countrymen were in the very act of raising the body of their comrade when a division of the civic watch rushed into the court in close order and through the passage near which the fight for the girl had arisen, thus stopping the way against those who were about to escape, since all who wished to get out of the court into the open street must pass through the doorway into which Klea had been forced by the horseman. Every other exit from this second court of the citadel led into the strictly guarded gardens and buildings of the palace itself.

The noisy strife round Klea, and the cry of the wounded man had attracted the watch; the Cypriotes and the maiden soon found themselves surrounded, and they were conducted through a narrow side passage into the court-yard of the prison. After a short enquiry the men who had been taken were allowed to return under an escort to their own phalanx, and Klea gladly followed the commander of the watch to a less brilliantly illuminated part of the prison-yard, for in him she had recognized at once Serapion's brother Glaucus, and he in her the daughter of the man who had done and suffered so much for his father's sake; besides they had often exchanged greetings and a few words in the temple of Serapis.

"All that is in my power," said Glaucus—a man somewhat taller but not so broadly built as his brother—when he had read the recluse's note and when Klea had answered a number of questions, "all that is in my power I will gladly do for you and your sister, for I do not forget all that I owe to your father; still I cannot but regret that you have incurred such risk, for it is always hazardous for a pretty young girl to venture into this palace at a late hour, and particularly just now, for the courts are swarming not only with Philometor's fighting men but with those of his brother, who have come here for their sovereign's birthday festival. The people have been liberally entertained, and the soldier who has been sacrificing to Dionysus seizes the gifts of Eros and Aphrodite wherever he may find them. I will at once take charge of my brother's letter to the Roman Publius Cornelius Scipio, but when you have received his answer you will do well to let yourself be escorted to my wife or my sister, who both live in the city, and to remain till to-morrow morning with one or the other. Here you cannot remain a minute unmolested while I am away— Where now—Aye! The only safe shelter I can offer you is the prison down there; the room where they lock up the subaltern officers when they have committed any offence is quite unoccupied, and I will conduct you thither. It is always kept clean, and there is a bench in it too."

Klea followed her friend who, as his hasty demeanor plainly showed, had been interrupted in important business. In a few steps they reached the prison; she begged Glaucus to bring her the Roman's answer as quickly as possible, declared herself quite ready to remain in the dark—since she perceived that the light of a lamp might betray her, and she was not afraid of the dark—and suffered herself to be locked in.

As she heard the iron bolt creak in its brass socket a shiver ran through her, and although the room in which she found herself was neither worse nor smaller than that in which she and her sister lived in the temple, still it oppressed her, and she even felt as if an indescribable something hindered her breathing as she said to herself that she was locked in and no longer free to come and to go. A dim light penetrated into her prison through the single barred window that opened on to the court, and she could see a little bench of palm-branches on which she sat down to seek the repose she so sorely needed. All sense of discomfort gradually vanished before the new feeling of rest and refreshment, and pleasant hopes and anticipations were just beginning to mingle themselves with the remembrance of the horrors she had just experienced when suddenly there was a stir and a bustle just in front of the prison—and she could hear, outside, the clatter of harness and words of command. She rose from her seat and saw that about twenty horsemen, whose golden helmets and armor reflected the light of the lanterns, cleared the wide court by driving the men before them, as the flames drive the game from a fired hedge, and by forcing them into a second court from which again they proceeded to expel them. At least Klea could hear them shouting 'In the king's name' there as they had before done close to her. Presently the horsemen returned and placed themselves, ten and ten, as guards at each of the passages leading into the court. It was not without interest that Klea looked on at this scene which was perfectly new to her; and when one of the fine horses, dazzled by the light of the lanterns, turned restive and shied, leaping and rearing and threatening his rider with a fall—when the horseman checked and soothed it, and brought it to a stand-still—the Macedonian warrior was transfigured in her eyes to Publius, who no doubt could manage a horse no less well than this man.

No sooner was the court completely cleared of men by the mounted guard than a new incident claimed Klea's attention. First she heard footsteps in the room adjoining her prison, then bright streaks of light fell through the cracks of the slight partition which divided her place of retreat from the other room, then the two window-openings close to hers were closed with heavy shutters, then seats or benches were dragged about and various objects were laid upon a table, and finally the door of the adjoining room was thrown open and slammed to again so violently, that the door which closed hers and the bench near which she was standing trembled and jarred.

At the same moment a deep sonorous voice called out with a loud and hearty shout of laughter:

"A mirror—give me a mirror, Eulaeus. By heaven! I do not look much like prison fare—more like a man in whose strong brain there is no lack of deep schemes, who can throttle his antagonist with a grip of his fist, and who is prompt to avail himself of all the spoil that comes in his way, so that he may compress the pleasures of a whole day into every hour, and enjoy them to the utmost! As surely as my name is Euergetes my uncle Antiochus was right in liking to mix among the populace. The splendid puppets who surround us kings, and cover every portion of their own bodies in wrappings and swaddling bands, also stifle the expression of every genuine sentiment; and it is enough to turn our brain to reflect that, if we would not be deceived, every word that we hear—and, oh dear! how many words we must needs hear-must be pondered in our minds. Now, the mob on the contrary—who think themselves beautifully dressed in a threadbare cloth hanging round their brown loins—are far better off. If one of them says to another of his own class—a naked wretch who wears about him everything he happens to possess—that he is a dog, he answers with a blow of his fist in the other's face, and what can be plainer than that! If on the other hand he tells him he is a splendid fellow, he believes it without reservation, and has a perfect right to believe it.

"Did you see how that stunted little fellow with a snub-nose and bandy-legs, who is as broad as he is long, showed all his teeth in a delighted grin when I praised his steady hand? He laughs just like a hyena, and every respectable father of a family looks on the fellow as a god- forsaken monster; but the immortals must think him worth something to have given him such magnificent grinders in his ugly mouth, and to have preserved him mercifully for fifty years—for that is about the rascal's age. If that fellow's dagger breaks he can kill his victim with those teeth, as a fox does a duck, or smash his bones with his fist."

"But, my lord," replied Eulaeus dryly and with a certain matter-of-fact gravity to King Euergetes—for he it was who had come with him into the room adjoining Klea's retreat, "the dry little Egyptian with the thin straight hair is even more trustworthy and tougher and nimbler than his companion, and, so far, more estimable. One flings himself on his prey with a rush like a block of stone hurled from a roof, but the other, without being seen, strikes his poisoned fang into his flesh like an adder hidden in the sand. The third, on whom I had set great hopes, was beheaded the day before yesterday without my knowledge; but the pair whom you have condescended to inspect with your own eyes are sufficient. They must use neither dagger nor lance, but they will easily achieve their end with slings and hooks and poisoned needles, which leave wounds that resemble the sting of an adder. We may safely depend on these fellows."

Once more Euergetes laughed loudly, and exclaimed: What criticism! Exactly as if these blood-hounds were tragic actors of which one could best produce his effects by fire and pathos, and the other by the subtlety of his conception. I call that an unprejudiced judgment. And why should not a man be great even as a murderer? From what hangman's noose did you drag out the neck of one, and from what headsman's block did you rescue the other when you found them?

"It is a lucky hour in which we first see something new to us, and, by Heracles! I never before in the whole course of my life saw such villains as these. I do not regret having gone to see them and talked to them as if I were their equal. Now, take this torn coat off me, and help me to undress. Before I go to the feast I will take a hasty plunge in my bath, for I twitch in every limb, I feel as if I had got dirty in their company.

"There lie my clothes and my sandals; strap them on for me, and tell me as you do it how you lured the Roman into the toils."

Klea could hear every word of this frightful conversation, and clasped her hand over her brow with a shudder, for she found it difficult to believe in the reality of the hideous images that it brought before her mind. Was she awake or was she a prey to some horrid dream?

She hardly knew, and, indeed, she scarcely understood half of all she heard till the Roman's name was mentioned. She felt as if the point of a thin, keen knife was being driven obliquely through her brain from right to left, as it now flashed through her mind that it was against him, against Publius, that the wild beasts, disguised in human form, were directed by Eulaeus, and face to face with this—the most hideous, the most incredible of horrors—she suddenly recovered the full use of her senses. She softly slipped close to that rift in the partition through which the broadest beam of light fell into the room, put her ear close to it, and drank in, with fearful attention, word for word the report made by the eunuch to his iniquitous superior, who frequently interrupted him with remarks, words of approval or a short laugh-drank them in, as a man perishing in the desert drinks the loathsome waters of a salt pool.

And what she heard was indeed well fitted to deprive her of her senses, but the more definite the facts to which the words referred that she could overhear, the more keenly she listened, and the more resolutely she collected her thoughts. Eulaeus had used her own name to induce the Roman to keep an assignation at midnight in the desert close to the Apis-tombs. He repeated the words that he had written to this effect on a tile, and which requested Publius to come quite alone to the spot indicated, since she dare not speak with him in the temple. Finally he was invited to write his answer on the other side of the square of clay. As Klea heard these words, put into her own mouth by a villain, she could have sobbed aloud heartily with anguish, shame, and rage; but the point now was to keep her ears wide open, for Euergetes asked his odious tool:

"And what was the Roman's answer?" Eulaeus must have handed the tile to the king, for he laughed loudly again, and cried out:

"So he will walk into the trap—will arrive by half an hour after midnight at the latest, and greets Klea from her sister Irene. He carries on love-making and abduction wholesale, and buys water-bearers by the pair, like doves in the market or sandals in a shoe maker's stall. Only see how the simpleton writes Greek; in these few words there are two mistakes, two regular schoolboys' blunders.

"The fellow must have had a very pleasant day of it, since he must have been reckoning on a not unsuccessful evening—but the gods have an ugly habit of clenching the hand with which they have long caressed their favorites, and striking him with their fist.

"Amalthea's horn has been poured out on him today; first he snapped up, under my very nose, my little Hebe, the Irene of Irenes, whom I hope to-morrow to inherit from him; then he got the gift of my best Cyrenaan horses, and at the same time the flattering assurance of my valuable friendship; then he had audience of my fair sister—and it goes more to the heart of a republican than you would believe when crowned heads are graciously disposed towards him—finally the sister of his pretty sweetheart invites him to an assignation, and she, if you and Zoe speak the truth, is a beauty in the grand style. Now these are really too many good things for one inhabitant of this most stingily provided world; and in one single day too, which, once begun, is so soon ended; and justice requires that we should lend a helping hand to destiny, and cut off the head of this poppy that aspires to rise above its brethren; the thousands who have less good fortune than he would otherwise have great cause to complain of neglect."

"I am happy to see you in such good humor," said Eulaeus.

"My humor is as may be," interrupted the king. "I believe I am only whistling a merry tune to keep up my spirits in the dark. If I were on more familiar terms with what other men call fear I should have ample reason to be afraid; for in the quail-fight we have gone in for I have wagered a crown-aye, and more than that even. To-morrow only will decide whether the game is lost or won, but I know already to-day that I would rather see my enterprise against Philometor fail, with all my hopes of the double crown, than our plot against the life of the Roman; for I was a man before I was a king, and a man I should remain, if my throne, which now indeed stands on only two legs, were to crash under my weight.

"My sovereign dignity is but a robe, though the costliest, to be sure, of all garments. If forgiveness were any part of my nature I might easily forgive the man who should soil or injure that—but he who comes too near to Euergetes the man, who dares to touch this body, and the spirit it contains, or to cross it in its desires and purposes—him I will crush unhesitatingly to the earth, I will see him torn in pieces. Sentence is passed on the Roman, and if your ruffians do their duty, and if the gods accept the holocaust that I had slain before them at sunset for the success of my project, in a couple of hours Publius Cornelius Scipio will have bled to death.

"He is in a position to laugh at me—as a man—but I therefore—as a man —have the right, and—as a king—have the power, to make sure that that laugh shall be his last. If I could murder Rome as I can him how glad should I be! for Rome alone hinders me from being the greatest of all the great kings of our time; and yet I shall rejoice to-morrow when they tell me Publius Cornelius Scipio has been torn by wild beasts, and his body is so mutilated that his own mother could not recognize it more than if a messenger were to bring me the news that Carthage had broken the power of Rome."

Euergetes had spoken the last words in a voice that sounded like the roll of thunder as it growls in a rapidly approaching storm, louder, deeper, and more furious each instant. When at last he was silent Eulaeus said: "The immortals, my lord, will not deny you this happiness. The brave fellows whom you condescended to see and to talk to strike as certainly as the bolt of our father Zeus, and as we have learned from the Roman's horse-keeper where he has hidden Irene, she will no more elude your grasp than the crowns of Upper and Lower Egypt.—Now, allow me to put on your mantle, and then to call the body-guard that they may escort you as you return to your residence."

"One thing more," cried the king, detaining Eulaeus. "There are always troops by the Tombs of Apis placed there to guard the sacred places; may not they prove a hindrance to your friends?"

"I have withdrawn all the soldiers and armed guards to Memphis down to the last man," replied Eulaeus, and quartered them within the White Wall. Early tomorrow, before you proceed to business, they will be replaced by a stronger division, so that they may not prove a reinforcement to your brother's troops here if things come to fighting."

"I shall know how to reward your foresight," said Euergetes as Eulaeus quitted the room.

Again Klea heard a door open, and the sound of many hoofs on the pavement of the court-yard, and when she went, all trembling, up to the window, she saw Euergetes himself, and the powerfully knit horse that was led in for him. The tyrant twisted his hand in the mane of the restless and pawing steed, and Klea thought that the monstrous mass could never mount on to the horse's back without the aid of many men; but she was mistaken, for with a mighty spring the giant flung himself high in the air and on to the horse, and then, guiding his panting steed by the pressure of his knees alone, he bounded out of the prison-yard surrounded by his splendid train.

For some minutes the court-yard remained empty, then a man hurriedly crossed it, unlocked the door of the room where Klea was, and informed her that he was a subaltern under Glaucus, and had brought her a message from him.

"My lord," said the veteran soldier to the girl, "bid me greet you, and says that he found neither the Roman Publius Scipio, nor his friend the Corinthian at home. He is prevented from coming to you himself; he has his hands full of business, for soldiers in the service of both the kings are quartered within the White Wall, and all sorts of squabbles break out between them. Still, you cannot remain in this room, for it will shortly be occupied by a party of young officers who began the fray. Glaucus proposes for your choice that you should either allow me to conduct you to his wife or return to the temple to which you are attached. In the latter case a chariot shall convey you as far as the second tavern in Khakem on the borders of the desert-for the city is full of drunken soldiery. There you may probably find an escort if you explain to the host who you are. But the chariot must be back again in less than an hour, for it is one of the king's, and when the banquet is over there may be a scarcity of chariots."

"Yes—I will go back to the place I came from," said Klea eagerly, interrupting the messenger. "Take me at once to the chariot."

"Follow me, then," said the old man.

"But I have no veil," observed Klea, "and have only this thin robe on. Rough soldiers snatched my wrapper from my face, and my cloak from off my shoulders."

"I will bring you the captain's cloak which is lying here in the orderly's room, and his travelling-hat too; that will hide your face with its broad flap. You are so tall that you might be taken for a man, and that is well, for a woman leaving the palace at this hour would hardly pass unmolested. A slave shall fetch the things from your temple to-morrow. I may inform you that my master ordered me take as much care of you as if you were his own daughter. And he told me too—and I had nearly forgotten it—to tell you that your sister was carried off by the Roman, and not by that other dangerous man, you would know whom he meant. Now wait, pray, till I return; I shall not be long gone."

In a few minutes the guard returned with a large cloak in which he wrapped Klea, and a broad-brimmed travelling-hat which she pressed down on her head, and he then conducted her to that quarter of the palace where the king's stables were. She kept close to the officer, and was soon mounted on a chariot, and then conducted by the driver—who took her for a young Macedonian noble, who was tempted out at night by some assignation—as far as the second tavern on the road back to the Serapeum.

CHAPTER XIX.

While Klea had been listening to the conversation between Euergetes and Eulaeus, Cleopatra had been sitting in her tent, and allowing herself to be dressed with no less care than on the preceding evening, but in other garments.

It would seem that all had not gone so smoothly as she wished during the day, for her two tire-women had red eyes. Her lady-in-waiting, Zoe, was reading to her, not this time from a Greek philosopher but from a Greek translation of the Hebrew Psalms: a discussion as to their poetic merit having arisen a few days previously at the supper-table. Onias, the Israelite general, had asserted that these odes might be compared with those of Alcman or of Pindar, and had quoted certain passages that had pleased the queen. To-day she was not disposed for thought, but wanted something strange and out of the common to distract her mind, so she desired Zoe to open the book of the Hebrews, of which the translation was considered by the Hellenic Jews in Alexandria as an admirable work—nay, even as inspired by God himself; it had long been known to her through her Israelite friends and guests.

Cleopatra had been listening for about a quarter of an hour to Zoe's reading when the blast of a trumpet rang out on the steps which led up her tent, announcing a visitor of the male sex. The queen glanced angrily round, signed to her lady to stop reading, and exclaimed:

"I will not see my husband now! Go, Thais, and tell the eunuchs on the steps, that I beg Philometor not to disturb me just now. Go on, Zoe."

Ten more psalms had been read, and a few verses repeated twice or thrice by Cleopatra's desire, when the pretty Athenian returned with flaming cheeks, and said in an excited tone:

"It is not your husband, the king, but your brother Euergetes, who asks to speak with you."

"He might have chosen some other hour," replied Cleopatra, looking round at her maid. Thais cast down her eyes, and twitched the edge of her robe between her fingers as she addressed her mistress; but the queen, whom nothing could escape that she chose to see, and who was not to-day in the humor for laughing or for letting any indiscretion escape unreproved, went on at once in an incensed and cutting tone, raising her voice to a sharp pitch:

"I do not choose that my messengers should allow themselves to be detained, be it by whom it may—do you hear! Leave Me this instant and go to your room, and stay there till I want you to undress me this evening. Andromeda—do you hear, old woman?—you can bring my brother to me, and he will let you return quicker than Thais, I fancy. You need not leer at yourself in the glass, you cannot do anything to alter your wrinkles. My head-dress is already done. Give me that linen wrapper, Olympias, and then he may come! Why, there he is already! First you ask permission, brother, and then disdain to wait till it is given you."

"Longing and waiting," replied Euergetes, "are but an ill-assorted couple. I wasted this evening with common soldiers and fawning flatterers; then, in order to see a few noble countenances, I went into the prison, after that I hastily took a bath, for the residence of your convicts spoils one's complexion more, and in a less pleasant manner, than this little shrine, where everything looks and smells like Aphrodite's tiring-room; and now I have a longing to hear a few good words before supper-time comes."

"From my lips?" asked Cleopatra.

"There are none that can speak better, whether by the Nile or the Ilissus."

"What do you want of me?"

"I—of you?"

"Certainly, for you do not speak so prettily unless you want something."

"But I have already told you! I want to hear you say something wise, something witty, something soul-stirring."

"We cannot call up wit as we would a maid-servant. It comes unbidden, and the more urgently we press it to appear the more certainly it remains away."

"That may be true of others, but not of you who, even while you declare that you have no store of Attic salt, are seasoning your speech with it. All yield obedience to grace and beauty, even wit and the sharp-tongued Momus who mocks even at the gods."

"You are mistaken, for not even my own waiting-maids return in proper time when I commission them with a message to you."

"And may we not to be allowed to sacrifice to the Charites on the way to the temple of Aphrodite?"

"If I were indeed the goddess, those worshippers who regarded my hand-maidens as my equals would find small acceptance with me."

"Your reproof is perfectly just, for you are justified in requiring that all who know you should worship but one goddess, as the Jews do but one god. But I entreat you do not again compare yourself to the brainless Cyprian dame. You may be allowed to do so, so far as your grace is concerned; but who ever saw an Aphrodite philosophizing and reading serious books? I have disturbed you in grave studies no doubt; what is the book you are rolling up, fair Zoe?"

"The sacred book of the Jews, Sire," replied Zoe; "one that I know you do not love."

And you—who read Homer, Pindar, Sophocles, and Plato—do you like it?" asked Euergetes.

"I find passages in it which show a profound knowledge of life, and others of which no one can dispute the high poetic flight," replied Cleopatra. "Much of it has no doubt a thoroughly barbarian twang, and it is particularly in the Psalms—which we have now been reading, and which might be ranked with the finest hymns—that I miss the number and rhythm of the syllables, the observance of a fixed metre—in short, severity of form. David, the royal poet, was no less possessed by the divinity when he sang to his lyre than other poets have been, but he does not seem to have known that delight felt by our poets in overcoming the difficulties they have raised for themselves. The poet should slavishly obey the laws he lays down for himself of his own free-will, and subordinate to them every word, and yet his matter and his song should seem to float on a free and soaring wing. Now, even the original Hebrew text of the Psalms has no metrical laws."

"I could well dispense with them," replied Euergetes; "Plato too disdained to measure syllables, and I know passages in his works which are nevertheless full of the highest poetic beauty. Besides, it has been pointed out to me that even the Hebrew poems, like the Egyptian, follow certain rules, which however I might certainly call rhetorical rather than poetical. The first member in a series of ideas stands in antithesis to the next, which either re-states the former one in a new form or sets it in a clearer light by suggesting some contrast. Thus they avail themselves of the art of the orator—or indeed of the painter —who brings a light color into juxtaposition with a dark one, in order to increase its luminous effect. This method and style are indeed not amiss, and that was the least of all the things that filled me with aversion for this book, in which besides, there is many a proverb which may be pleasing to kings who desire to have submissive subjects, and to fathers who would bring up their sons in obedience to themselves and to the laws. Even mothers must be greatly comforted by them,—who ask no more than that their children may get through the world without being jostled or pushed, and unmolested if possible, that they may live longer than the oaks or ravens, and be blessed with the greatest possible number of descendants. Aye! these ordinances are indeed precious to those who accept them, for they save them the trouble of thinking for themselves. Besides, the great god of the Jews is said to have dictated all that this book contains to its writers, just as I dictate to Philippus, my hump- backed secretary, all that I want said. They regard everyone as a blasphemer and desecrator who thinks that anything written in that roll is erroneous, or even merely human. Plato's doctrines are not amiss, and yet Aristotle had criticised them severely and attempted to confute them. I myself incline to the views of the Stagyrite, you to those of the noble Athenian, and how many good and instructive hours we owe to our discussions over this difference of opinion! And how amusing it is to listen when the Platonists on the one hand and the Aristotelians on the other, among the busy threshers of straw in the Museum at Alexandria, fall together by the ears so vehemently that they would both enjoy flinging their metal cups at each others' heads—if the loss of the wine, which I pay for, were not too serious to bear. We still seek for truth; the Jews believe they possess it entirely.

"Even those among them who most zealously study our philosophers believe this; and yet the writers of this book know of nothing but actual present, and their god—who will no more endure another god as his equal than a citizen's wife will admit a second woman to her husband's house— is said to have created the world out of nothing for no other purpose but to be worshipped and feared by its inhabitants.

"Now, given a philosophical Jew who knows his Empedocles—and I grant there are many such in Alexandria, extremely keen and cultivated men— what idea can he form in his own mind of 'creation out of nothing?' Must he not pause to think very seriously when he remembers the fundamental axiom that 'out of nothing, nothing can come,' and that nothing which has once existed can ever be completely annihilated? At any rate the necessary deduction must be that the life of man ends in that nothingness whence everything in existence has proceeded. To live and to die according to this book is not highly profitable. I can easily reconcile myself to the idea of annihilation, as a man who knows how to value a dreamless sleep after a day brimful of enjoyment—as a man who if he must cease to be Euergetes would rather spring into the open jaws of nothingness—but as a philosopher, no, never!"

"You, it is true," replied the queen, "cannot help measuring all and everything by the intellectual standard exclusively; for the gods, who endowed you with gifts beyond a thousand others, struck with blindness or deafness that organ which conveys to our minds any religious or moral sentiment. If that could see or hear, you could no more exclude the conviction that these writings are full of the deepest purport than I can, nor doubt that they have a powerful hold on the mind of the reader.

"They fetter their adherents to a fixed law, but they take all bitterness out of sorrow by teaching that a stern father sends us suffering which is represented as being sometimes a means of education, and sometimes a punishment for transgressing a hard and clearly defined law. Their god, in his infallible but stern wisdom, sets those who cling to him on an evil and stony path to prove their strength, and to let them at last reach the glorious goal which is revealed to them from the beginning."

"How strange such words as these sound in the mouth of a Greek," interrupted Euergetes. "You certainly must be repeating them after the son of the Jewish high-priest, who defends the cause of his cruel god with so much warmth and skill."

"I should have thought," retorted Cleopatra, "that this overwhelming figure of a god would have pleased you, of all men; for I know of no weakness in you. Quite lately Dositheos, the Jewish centurion—a very learned man— tried to describe to my husband the one great god to whom his nation adheres with such obstinate fidelity, but I could not help thinking of our beautiful and happy gods as a gay company of amorous lords and pleasure-loving ladies, and comparing them with this stern and powerful being who, if only he chose to do it, might swallow them all up, as Chronos swallowed his own children."

"That," exclaimed Euergetes, "is exactly what most provokes me in this superstition. It crushes our light-hearted pleasure in life, and whenever I have been reading the book of the Hebrews everything has come into my mind that I least like to think of. It is like an importunate creditor that reminds us of our forgotten debts, and I love pleasure and hate an importunate reminder. And you, pretty one, life blooms for you—"

"But I," interrupted Cleopatra, "I can admire all that is great; and does it not seem a bold and grand thing even to you, that the mighty idea that it is one single power that moves and fills the world, should be freely and openly declared in the sacred writings of the Jews—an idea which the Egyptians carefully wrap up and conceal, which the priests of the Nile only venture to divulge to the most privileged of those who are initiated into their mysteries, and which—though the Greek philosophers indeed have fearlessly uttered it—has never been introduced by any Hellene into the religion of the people? If you were not so averse to the Hebrew nation, and if you, like my husband and myself, had diligently occupied yourself with their concerns and their belief you would be juster to them and to their scriptures, and to the great creating and preserving spirit, their god—"

"You are confounding this jealous and most unamiable and ill-tempered tyrant of the universe with the Absolute of Aristotle!" cried Euergetes; "he stigmatises most of what you and I and all rational Greeks require for the enjoyment of life as sin—sin upon sin. And yet if my easily persuadable brother governed at Alexandria, I believe the shrewd priests might succeed in stamping him as a worshipper of that magnified schoolmaster, who punishes his untutored brood with fire and torment."

"I cannot deny," replied Cleopatra, "that even to me the doctrine of the Jews has something very fearful in it, and that to adopt it seems to me tantamount to confiscating all the pleasures of life.—But enough of such things, which I should no more relish as a daily food than you do. Let us rejoice in that we are Hellenes, and let us now go to the banquet. I fear you have found a very unsatisfactory substitute for what you sought in coming up here."

"No—no. I feel strangely excited to-day, and my work with Aristarchus would have led to no issue. It is a pity that we should have begun to talk of that barbarian rubbish; there are so many other subjects more pleasing and more cheering to the mind. Do you remember how we used to read the great tragedians and Plato together?"

"And how you would often interrupt our tutor Agatharchides in his lectures on geography, to point out some mistake! Did you prosecute those studies in Cyrene?"

"Of course. It really is a pity, Cleopatra, that we should no longer live together as we did formerly. There is no one, not even Aristarchus, with whom I find it more pleasant and profitable to converse and discuss than with you. If only you had lived at Athens in the time of Pericles, who knows if you might not have been his friend instead of the immortal Aspasia. This Memphis is certainly not the right place for you; for a few months in the year you ought to come to Alexandria, which has now risen to be superior to Athens."

"I do not know you to-day!" exclaimed Cleopatra, gazing at her brother in astonishment. "I have never heard you speak so kindly and brotherly since the death of my mother. You must have some great request to make of us."

"You see how thankless a thing it is for me to let my heart speak for once, like other people. I am like the boy in the fable when the wolf came! I have so often behaved in an unbrotherly fashion that when I show the aspect of a brother you think I have put on a mask. If I had had anything special to ask of you I should have waited till to-morrow, for in this part of the country even a blind beggar does not like to refuse his lame comrade anything on his birthday."

"If only we knew what you wish for! Philometor and I would do it more than gladly, although you always want something monstrous. Our performance to-morrow will—at any rate—but—Zoe, pray be good enough to retire with the maids; I have a few words to say to my brother alone."

As soon as the queen's ladies had withdrawn, she went on:

"It is a real grief to use, but the best part of the festival in honor of your birthday will not be particularly successful, for the priests of Serapis spitefully refuse us the Hebe about whom Lysias has made us so curious. Asclepiodorus, it would seem, keeps her in concealment, and carries his audacity so far as to tell us that someone has carried her off from the temple. He insinuates that we have stolen her, and demands her restitution in the name of all his associates."

"You are doing the man an injustice; our dove has followed the lure of a dove-catcher who will not allow me to have her, and who is now billing and cooing with her in his own nest. I am cheated, but I can scarcely be angry with the Roman, for his claim was of older standing than mine."

"The Roman?" asked Cleopatra, rising from her seat and turning pale. "But that is impossible. You are making common cause with Eulaeus, and want to set me against Publius Scipio. At the banquet last night you showed plainly enough your ill-feeling against him."

"You seem to feel more warmly towards him. But before I prove to you that I am neither lying nor joking, may I enquire what has this man, this many-named Publius Cornelius Scipio Nasica, to recommend him above any handsome well-grown Macedonian, who is resolute in my cause, in the whole corps of your body guard, excepting his patrician pride? He is as bitter and ungenial as a sour apple, and all the very best that you—a subtle thinker, a brilliant and cultivated philosopher—can find to say is no more appreciated by his meanly cultivated intellect than the odes of Sappho by a Nubian boatman."

"It is exactly for that," cried the queen, "that I value him; he is different from all of us; we who—how shall I express myself—who always think at second-hand, and always set our foot in the rut trodden by the master of the school we adhere to; who squeeze our minds into the moulds that others have carved out, and when we speak hesitate to step beyond the outlines of those figures of rhetoric which we learned at school! You have burst these bonds, but even your mighty spirit still shows traces of them. Publius Scipio, on the contrary, thinks and sees and speaks with perfect independence, and his upright sense guides him to the truth without any trouble or special training. His society revives me like the fresh air that I breathe when I come out into the open air from the temple filled with the smoke of incense—like the milk and bread which a peasant offered us during our late excursion to the coast, after we had been living for a year on nothing but dainties."

"He has all the admirable characteristics of a child!" interrupted Euergetes. "And if that is all that appears estimable to you in the Roman your son may soon replace the great Cornelius."

"Not soon! no, not till he shall have grown older than you are, and a man, a thorough man, from the crown of his head to the sole of his foot, for such a man is Publius! I believe—nay, I am sure—that he is incapable of any mean action, that he could not be false in word or even in look, nor feign a sentiment be did not feel."

"Why so vehement, sister? So much zeal is quite unnecessary on this occasion! You know well enough that I have my easy days, and that this excitement is not good for you; nor has the Roman deserved that you should be quite beside yourself for his sake. The fellow dared in my presence to look at you as Paris might at Helen before he carried her off, and to drink out of your cup; and this morning he no doubt did not contradict what he conveyed to you last night with his eyes—nay, perhaps by his words. And yet, scarcely an hour before, he had been to the Necropolis to bear his sweetheart away from the temple of the gloomy Serapis into that of the smiling Eros."

"You shall prove this!" cried the queen in great excitement. "Publius is my friend—"

"And I am yours!"

"You have often proved the reverse, and now again with lies and cheating—"

"You seem," interrupted Euergetes, "to have learned from your unphilosophical favorite to express your indignation with extraordinary frankness; to-day however I am, as I have said, as gentle as a kitten—"

"Euergetes and gentleness!" cried Cleopatra with a forced laugh. "No, you only step softly like a cat when she is watching a bird, and your gentleness covers some ruthless scheme, which we shall find out soon enough to our cost. You have been talking with Eulaeus to-day; Eulaeus, who fears and hates Publius, and it seems to me that you have hatched some conspiracy against him; but if you dare to cast a single stone in his path, to touch a single hair of his head, I will show you that even a weak woman can be terrible. Nemesis and the Erinnyes from Alecto to Megaera, the most terrible of all the gods, are women!"

Cleopatra had hissed rather than spoken these words, with her teeth set with rage, and had raised her small fist to threaten her brother; but Euergetes preserved a perfect composure till she had ceased speaking. Then he took a step closer to her, crossed his arms over his breast, and asked her in the deepest bass of his fine deep voice:

"Are you idiotically in love with this Publius Cornelius Scipio Nasica, or do you purpose to make use of him and his kith and kin in Rome against me?"

Transported with rage, and without blenching in the least at her brother's piercing gaze, she hastily retorted: "Up to this moment only the first perhaps—for what is my husband to me? But if you go on as you have begun I shall begin to consider how I may make use of his influence and of his liking for me, on the shores of the Tiber."

"Liking!" cried Euergetes, and he laughed so loud and violently that Zoe, who was listening at the tent door, gave a little scream, and Cleopatra drew back a step. "And to think that you—the most prudent of the prudent—who can hear the dew fall and the grass grow, and smell here in Memphis the smoke of every fire that is lighted in Alexandria or in Syria or even in Rome—that you, my mother's daughter, should be caught over head and ears by a broad-shouldered lout, for all the world like a clumsy town-girl or a wench at a loom. This ignorant Adonis, who knows so well how to make use of his own strange and resolute personality, and of the power that stands in his background, thinks no more of the hearts he sets in flames than I of the earthen jar out of which water is drawn when I am thirsty. You think to make use of him by the Tiber; but he has anticipated you, and learns from you all that is going on by the Nile and everything they most want to know in the Senate.

"You do not believe me, for no one ever is ready to believe anything that can diminish his self-esteem—and why should you believe me? I frankly confess that I do not hesitate to lie when I hope to gain more by untruth than by that much-belauded and divine truth, which, according to your favorite Plato, is allied to all earthly beauty; but it is often just as useless as beauty itself, for the useful and the beautiful exclude each other in a thousand cases, for ten when they coincide. There, the gong is sounding for the third time. If you care for plain proof that the Roman, only an hour before he visited you this morning, had our little Hebe carried off from the temple, and conveyed to the house of Apollodorus, the sculptor, at Memphis, you have only to come to see me in my rooms early to-morrow after the first morning sacrifice. You will at any rate wish to come and congratulate me; bring your children with you, as I propose making them presents. You might even question the Roman himself at the banquet to-day, but he will hardly appear, for the sweetest gifts of Eros are bestowed at night, and as the temple of Serapis is closed at sunset Publius has never yet seen his Irene in the evening. May I expect you and the children after morning sacrifice?"

Before Cleopatra had time to answer this question another trumpet-blast was heard, and she exclaimed: "That is Philometor, come to fetch us to the banquet. I will ere long give the Roman the opportunity of defending himself, though—in spite of your accusations—I trust him entirely. This morning I asked him solemnly whether it was true that he was in love with his friend's charming Hebe, and he denied it in his firm and manly way, and his replies were admirable and worthy of the noblest mind, when I ventured to doubt his sincerity. He takes truth more seriously than you do. He regards it not only as beautiful and right to be truthful, he says, but as prudent too; for lies can only procure us a small short- lived advantage, as transitory as the mists of night which vanish as soon as the sun appears, while truth is like the sunlight itself, which as often as it is dimmed by clouds reappears again and again. And, he says, what makes a liar so particularly contemptible in his eyes is, that to attain his end, he must be constantly declaring and repeating the horror he has of those who are and do the very same thing as he himself. The ruler of a state cannot always be truthful, and I often have failed in truth; but my intercourse with Publius has aroused much that is good in me, and which had been slumbering with closed eyes; and if this man should prove to be the same as all the rest of you, then I will follow your road, Euergetes, and laugh at virtue and truth, and set the busts of Aristippus and Strato on the pedestals where those of Zeno and Antisthenes now stand."

"You mean to have the busts of the philosophers moved again?" asked King Philometor, who, as he entered the tent, had heard the queen's last words. "And Aristippus is to have the place of honor? I have no objection—though he teaches that man must subjugate matter and not become subject to it.—["Mihi res, non me rebus subjungere."]—This indeed is easier to say than to do, and there is no man to whom it is more impossible than to a king who has to keep on good terms with Greeks and Egyptians, as we have, and with Rome as well. And besides all this to avoid quarrelling with a jealous brother, who shares our kingdom! If men could only know how much they would have to do as kings only in reading and writing, they would take care never to struggle for a crown! Up to this last half hour I have been examining and deciding applications and petitions. Have you got through yours, Euergetes? Even more had accumulated for you than for us."

"All were settled in an hour," replied the other promptly. "My eye is quicker than the mouth of your reader, and my decisions commonly consist of three words while you dictate long treatises to your scribes. So I had done when you had scarcely begun, and yet I could tell you at once, if it were not too tedious a matter, every single case that has come before me for months, and explain it in all its details."

"That I could not indeed," said Philometor modestly, "but I know and admire your swift intelligence and accurate memory."

"You see I am more fit for a king than you are;" laughed Euergetes. "You are too gentle and debonair for a throne! Hand over your government to me. I will fill your treasury every year with gold. I beg you now, come to Alexandria with Cleopatra for good, and share with me the palace and the gardens in the Bruchion. I will nominate your little Philopator heir to the throne, for I have no wish to contract a permanent tie with any woman, as Cleopatra belongs to you. This is a bold proposal, but reflect, Philometor, if you were to accept it, how much time it would give you for your music, your disputations with the Jews, and all your other favorite occupations."

"You never know how far you may go with your jest!" interrupted Cleopatra. "Besides, you devote quite as much time to your studies in philology and natural history as he does to music and improving conversations with his learned friends."

"Just so," assented Philometor, "and you may be counted among the sages of the Museum with far more reason than I."

"But the difference between us," replied Euergetes, "is that I despise all the philosophical prattlers and rubbish-collectors in Alexandria almost to the point of hating them, while for science I have as great a passion as for a lover. You, on the contrary, make much of the learned men, but trouble yourself precious little about science."

"Drop the subject, pray," begged Cleopatra. "I believe that you two have never yet been together for half an hour without Euergetes having begun some dispute, and Philometor having at last given in, to pacify him. Our guests must have been waiting for us a long time. Had Publius Scipio made his appearance?"

"He had sent to excuse himself," replied the king as he scratched the poll of Cleopatra's parrot, parting its feathers with the tips of his fingers. "Lysias, the Corinthian, is sitting below, and he says he does not know where his friend can be gone."

"But we know very well," said Euergetes, casting an ironical glance at the queen. "It is pleasant to be with Philometor and Cleopatra, but better still with Eros and Hebe. Sister, you look pale—shall I call for Zoe?"

Cleopatra shook her head in negation, but she dropped into a seat, and sat stooping, with her head bowed over her knees as if she were dreadfully tired. Euergetes turned his back on her, and spoke to his brother of indifferent subjects, while she drew lines, some straight and some crooked, with her fan-stick through the pile of the soft rug on the floor, and sat gazing thoughtfully at her feet. As she sat thus her eye was caught by her sandals, richly set with precious stones, and the slender toes she had so often contemplated with pleasure; but now the sight of them seemed to vex her, for in obedience to a swift impulse she loosened the straps, pushed off her right sandal with her left foot, kicked it from her, and said, turning to her husband:

"It is late and I do not feel well, and you may sup without me."

"By the healing Isis!" exclaimed Philometor, going up to her. "You look suffering. Shall I send for the physicians? Is it really nothing more than your usual headache? The gods be thanked! But that you should be unwell just to-day! I had so much to say to you; and the chief thing of all was that we are still a long way from completeness in our preparations for our performance. If this luckless Hebe were not—"

"She is in good hands," interrupted Euergetes. "The Roman, Publius Scipio, has taken her to a place of safety; perhaps in order to present her to me to morrow morning in return for the horses from Cyrene which I sent him to-day. How brightly your eyes sparkle, sister—with joy no doubt at this good idea. This evening, I dare say he is rehearsing the little one in her part that she may perform it well to-morrow. If we are mistaken—if Publius is ungrateful and proposes keeping the dove, then Thais, your pretty Athenian waiting-woman, may play the part of Hebe. What do you think of that suggestion, Cleopatra?"

"That I forbid such jesting with me!" cried the queen vehemently. "No one has any consideration for me—no one pities me, and I suffer fearfully! Euergetes scorns me—you, Philometor, would be glad to drag me down! If only the banquet is not interfered with, and so long as nothing spoils your pleasure!—Whether I die or no, no one cares!"

With these words the queen burst into tears, and roughly pushed away her husband as he endeavored to soothe her. At last she dried her eyes, and said: "Go down-the guests are waiting."

"Immediately, my love," replied Philometor. "But one thing I must tell you, for I know that it will arouse your sympathy. The Roman read to you the petition for pardon for Philotas, the chief of the Chrematistes and 'relative of the king,' which contains such serious charges against Eulaeus. I was ready with all my heart to grant your wish and to pardon the man who is the father of these miserable water-bearers; but, before having the decree drawn up, I had the lists of the exiles to the gold- mines carefully looked through, and there it was discovered that Philotas and his wife have both been dead more than half a year. Death has settled this question, and I cannot grant to Publius the first service he has asked of me—asked with great urgency too. I am sorry for this, both for his sake and for that of poor Philotas, who was held in high esteem by our mother."

"May the ravens devour them!" answered Cleopatra, pressing her forehead against the ivory frame which surrounded the stuffed back of her seat. "Once more I beg of you excuse me from all further speech." This time the two kings obeyed her wishes. When Euergetes offered her his hand she said with downcast eyes, and poking her fan-stick into the wool of the carpet:

"I will visit you early to-morrow."

"After the first sacrifice," added Euergetes. "If I know you well, something that you will then hear will please you greatly; very greatly indeed, I should think. Bring the children with you; that I ask of you as a birthday request."

CHAPTER XX.

The royal chariot in which Klea was standing, wrapped in the cloak and wearing the hat of the captain of the civic guard, went swiftly and without stopping through the streets of Memphis. As long as she saw houses with lighted windows on each side of the way, and met riotous soldiers and quiet citizens going home from the taverns, or from working late in their workshops, with lanterns in their hands or carried by their slaves—so long her predominant feeling was one of hatred to Publius; and mixed with this was a sentiment altogether new to her—a sentiment that made her blood boil, and her heart now stand still and then again beat wildly—the thought that he might be a wretched deceiver. Had he not attempted to entrap one of them—whether her sister or herself it was all the same—wickedly to betray her, and to get her into his power!

"With me," thought she, "he could not hope to gain his evil ends, and when he saw that I knew how to protect myself he lured the poor unresisting child away with him, in order to ruin her and to drag her into shame and misery. Just like Rome herself, who seizes on one country after another to make them her own, so is this ruthless man. No sooner had that villain Eulaeus' letter reached him, than he thought himself justified in believing that I too was spellbound by a glance from his eyes, and would spread my wings to fly into his arms; and so he put out his greedy hand to catch me too, and threw aside the splendor and delights of a royal banquet to hurry by night out into the desert, and to risk a hideous death—for the avenging deities still punish the evildoer."

By this time she was shrouded in total darkness, for the moon was still hidden by black clouds. Memphis was already behind her, and the chariot was passing through a tall-stemmed palm-grove, where even at mid-day deep shades intermingled with the sunlight. When, just at this spot, the thought once more pierced her soul that the seducer was devoted to death, she felt as though suddenly a bright glaring light had flashed up in her and round her, and she could have broken out into a shout of joy like one who, seeking retribution for blood, places his foot at last on the breast of his fallen foe. She clenched her teeth tightly and grasped her girdle, in which she had stuck the knife given her by the smith.

If the charioteer by her side had been Publius, she would have stabbed him to the heart with the weapon with delight, and then have thrown herself under the horses' hoofs and the brazen wheels of the chariot.

But no! Still more gladly would she have found him dying in the desert, and before his heart had ceased to beat have shouted in his ear how much she hated him; and then, when his breast no longer heaved a breath—then she would have flung herself upon him, and have kissed his dimmed eyes.

Her wildest thoughts of vengeance were as inseparable from tender pity and the warmest longings of a heart overflowing with love, as the dark waters of a river are from the brighter flood of a stream with which it has recently mingled. All the passionate impulses which had hitherto been slumbering in her soul were set free, and now raised their clamorous voices as she was whirled across the desert through the gloom of night. The wishes roused in her breast by her hatred appealing to her on one side and her love singing in her ear, in tempting flute-tones, on the other, jostled and hustled one another, each displacing the other as they crowded her mind in wild confusion. As she proceeded on her journey she felt that she could have thrown herself like a tigress on her victim, and yet—like an outcast woman—have flung herself at Publius' knees in supplication for the love that was denied her. She had lost all idea of time and distance, and started as from a wild and bewildering dream when the chariot suddenly halted, and the driver said in his rough tones:

"Here we are, I must turn back again."

She shuddered, drew the cloak more closely round her, sprang out on to the road, and stood there motionless till the charioteer said:

"I have not spared my horses, my noble gentleman. Won't you give me something to get a drop of wine?" Klea's whole possessions were two silver drachma, of which she herself owned one and the other belonged to Irene. On the last anniversary but one of his mother's death, the king had given at the temple a sum to be divided among all the attendants, male and female, who served Serapis, and a piece of silver had fallen to the share of herself and her sister. Klea had them both about her in a little bag, which also contained a ring that her mother had given her at parting, and the amulet belonging to Serapion. The girl took out the two silver coins and gave them to the driver, who, after testing the liberal gift with his fingers, cried out as he turned his horses:

"A pleasant night to you, and may Aphrodite and all the Loves be favorable!"

"Irene's drachma!" muttered Klea to herself, as the chariot rolled away. The sweet form of her sister rose before her mind; she recalled the hour when the girl—still but a child—had entrusted it to her, because she lost everything unless Klea took charge of it for her.

"Who will watch her and care for her now?" she asked herself, and she stood thinking, trying to defend herself against the wild wishes which again began to stir in her, and to collect her scattered thoughts. She had involuntarily avoided the beam of light which fell across the road from the tavern-window, and yet she could not help raising her eyes and looking along it, and she found herself looking through the darkness which enveloped her, straight into the faces of two men whose gaze was directed to the very spot where she was standing. And what faces they were that she saw! One, a fat face, framed in thick hair and a short, thick and ragged beard, was of a dusky brown and as coarse and brutal as the other was smooth, colorless and lean, cruel and crafty. The eyes of the first of these ruffians were prominent, weak and bloodshot, with a fixed glassy stare, while those of the other seemed always to be on the watch with a restless and uneasy leer.

These were Euergetes' assassins—they must be! Spellbound with terror and revulsion she stood quite still, fearing only that the ruffians might hear the beating of her heart, for she felt as if it were a hammer swung up and down in an empty space, and beating with loud echoes, now in her bosom and now in her throat.

"The young gentleman must have gone round behind the tavern—he knows the shortest way to the 'tombs. Let us go after him, and finish off the business at once," said the broad-shouldered villain in a hoarse whisper that broke down every now and then, and which seemed to Klea even more repulsive than the monster's face.

"So that he may hear us go after him-stupid!" answered the other. "When he has been waiting for his sweetheart about a quarter of an hour I will call his name in a woman's voice, and at his first step towards the desert do you break his neck with the sand-bag. We have plenty of time yet, for it must still be a good half hour before midnight."

"So much the better," said the other. "Our wine-jar is not nearly empty yet, and we paid the lazy landlord for it in advance, before he crept into bed."

"You shall only drink two cups more," said the punier villain. "For this time we have to do with a sturdy fellow, Setnam is not with us now to lend a hand in the work, and the dead meat must show no gaping thrusts or cuts. My teeth are not like yours when you are fasting—even cooked food must not be too tough for them to chew it, now-a-days. If you soak yourself in drink and fail in your blow, and I am not ready with the poisoned stiletto the thing won't come off neatly. But why did not the Roman let his chariot wait?"

"Aye! why did he let it go away?" asked the other staring open-mouthed in the direction where the sound of wheels was still to be heard. His companion mean while laid his hand to his ear, and listened. Both were silent for a few minutes, then the thin one said:

"The chariot has stopped at the first tavern. So much the better. The Roman has valuable cattle in his shafts, and at the inn down there, there is a shed for horses. Here in this hole there is hardly a stall for an ass, and nothing but sour wine and mouldy beer. I don't like the rubbish, and save my coin for Alexandria and white Mariotic; that is strengthening and purifies the blood. For the present I only wish we were as well off as those horses; they will have plenty of time to recover their breath."

"Yes, plenty of time," answered the other with a broad grin, and then he with his companion withdrew into the room to fill his cup.

Klea too could hear that the chariot which had brought her hither, had halted at the farther tavern, but it did not occur to her that the driver had gone in to treat himself to wine with half of Irene's drachma. The horses should make up for the lost time, and they could easily do it, for when did the king's banquets ever end before midnight?

As soon as Plea saw that the assassins were filling their earthen cups, she slipped softly on tiptoe behind the tavern; the moon came out from behind the clouds for a few minutes, she sought and found the short way by the desert-path to the Apis-tombs, and hastened rapidly along it. She looked straight before her, for whenever she glanced at the road-side, and her eye was caught by some dried up shrub of the desert, silvery in the pale moonlight, she fancied she saw behind it the face of a murderer.

The skeletons of fallen beasts standing up out of the dust, and the bleached jawbones of camels and asses, which shone much whiter than the desert-sand on which they lay, seemed to have come to life and motion, and made her think of the tiger-teeth of the bearded ruffian.

The clouds of dust driven in her face by the warm west wind, which had risen higher, increased her alarm, for they were mingled with the colder current of the night-breeze; and again and again she felt as if spirits were driving her onwards with their hot breath, and stroking her face with their cold fingers. Every thing that her senses perceived was transformed by her heated imagination into a fearful something; but more fearful and more horrible than anything she heard, than any phantom that met her eye in the ghastly moonlight, were her own thoughts of what was to be done now, in the immediate future—of the fearful fate that threatened the Roman and Irene; and she was incapable of separating one from the other in her mind, for one influence alone possessed her, heart and soul: dread, dread; the same boundless, nameless, deadly dread—alike of mortal peril and irremediable shame, and of the airiest phantoms and the merest nothings.

A large black cloud floated slowly across the moon and utter darkness hid everything around, even the undefined forms which her imagination had turned to images of dread. She was forced to moderate her pace, and find her way, feeling each step; and just as to a child some hideous form that looms before him vanishes into nothingness when he covers his eyes with his hand, so the profound darkness which now enveloped her, suddenly released her soul from a hundred imaginary terrors.

She stood still, drew a deep breath, collected the whole natural force of her will, and asked herself what she could do to avert the horrid issue.

Since seeing the murderers every thought of revenge, every wish to punish the seducer with death, had vanished from her mind; one desire alone possessed her now—that of rescuing him, the man, from the clutches of these ravening beasts. Walking slowly onwards she repeated to herself every word she had heard that referred to Publius and Irene as spoken by Euergetes, Eulaeus, the recluse, and the assassins, and recalled every step she had taken since she left the temple; thus she brought herself back to the consciousness that she had come out and faced danger and endured terror, solely and exclusively for Irene's sake. The image of her sister rose clearly before her mind in all its bright charm, undimmed by any jealous grudge which, indeed, ever since her passion had held her in its toils had never for the smallest fraction of a minute possessed her.

Irene had grown up under her eye, sheltered by her care, in the sunshine of her love. To take care of her, to deny herself, and bear the severest fatigue for her had been her pleasure; and now as she appealed to her father—as she wont to do—as if he were present, and asked him in an inaudible cry: "Tell me, have I not done all for her that I could do?" and said to herself that he could not possibly answer her appeal but with assent, her eyes filled with tears; the bitterness and discontent which had lately filled her breast gradually disappeared, and a gentle, calm, refreshing sense of satisfaction came over her spirit, like a cooling breeze after a scorching day.

As she now again stood still, straining her eyes which were growing more accustomed to the darkness, to discover one of the temples at the end of the alley of sphinxes, suddenly and unexpectedly at her right hand a solemn and many-voiced hymn of lamentation fell upon her ear. This was from the priests of Osiris-Apis who were performing the sacred mysteries of their god, at midnight, on the roof of the temple. She knew the hymn well—a lament for the deceased Osiris which implored him with urgent supplication to break the power of death, to rise again, to bestow new light and new vitality on the world and on men, and to vouchsafe to all the departed a new existence.

The pious lament had a powerful effect on her excited spirit. Her parents too perhaps had passed through death, and were now taking part in the conduct of the destiny of the world and of men in union with the life giving God. Her breath came fast, she threw up her arms, and, for the first time since in her wrath she had turned her back on the holy of holies in the temple of Serapis, she poured forth her whole soul with passionate fervor in a deep and silent prayer for strength to fulfil her duty to the end,—for some sign to show her the way to save Irene from misfortune, and Publius from death. And as she prayed she felt no longer alone—no, it seemed to her that she stood face to face with the invincible Power which protects the good, in whom she now again had faith, though for Him she knew no name; as a daughter, pursued by foes, might clasp her powerful father's knees and claim his succor.

She had not stood thus with uplifted arms for many minutes when the moon, once more appearing, recalled her to herself and to actuality. She now perceived close to her, at hardly a hundred paces from where she stood, the line of sphinxes by the side of which lay the tombs of Apis near which she was to await Publius. Her heart began to beat faster again, and her dread of her own weakness revived. In a few minutes she must meet the Roman, and, involuntarily putting up her hand to smooth her hair, she was reminded that she still wore Glaucus' hat on her head and his cloak wrapped round her shoulders. Lifting up her heart again in a brief prayer for a calm and collected mind, she slowly arranged her dress and its folds, and as she did so the key of the tomb-cave, which she still had about her, fell under her hand. An idea flashed through her brain—she caught at it, and with hurried breath followed it out, till she thought she had now hit upon the right way to preserve from death the man who was so rich and powerful, who had given her nothing but taken everything from her, and to whom, nevertheless, she—the poor water- bearer whom he had thought to trifle with—could now bestow the most precious of the gifts of the immortals, namely, life.

Serapion had said, and she was willing to believe, that Publius was not base, and he certainly was not one of those who could prove ungrateful to a preserver. She longed to earn the right to demand something of him, and that could be nothing else but that he should give up her sister and bring Irene back to her.

When could it be that he had come to an understanding with the inexperienced and easily wooed maiden? How ready she must have been to clasp the hand held out to her by this man! Nothing surprised her in Irene, the child of the present; she could comprehend too that Irene's charm might quickly win the heart even of a grave and serious man.

And yet—in all the processions it was never Irene that he had gazed at, but always herself, and how came it to pass that he had given a prompt and ready assent to the false invitation to go out to meet her in the desert at midnight? Perhaps she was still nearer to his heart than Irene, and if gratitude drew him to her with fresh force then—aye then— he might perhaps woo her, and forget his pride and her lowly position, and ask her to be his wife.

She thought this out fully, but before she had reached the half circle enclosed by the Philosophers' busts the question occurred to her mind. And Irene?

Had she gone with him and quitted her without bidding her farewell because the young heart was possessed with a passionate love for Publius —who was indeed the most lovable of men? And he? Would he indeed, out of gratitude for what she hoped to do for him, make up his mind, if she demanded it, to make her Irene his wife—the poor but more than lovely daughter of a noble house?

And if this were possible, if these two could be happy in love and honor, should she Klea come between the couple to divide them? Should she jealously snatch Irene from his arms and carry her back to the gloomy temple which now—after she had fluttered awhile in sportive freedom in the sunny air—would certainly seem to her doubly sinister and unendurable? Should she be the one to plunge Irene into misery—Irene, her child, the treasure confided to her care, whom she had sworn to cherish?

"No, and again no," she said resolutely. "She was born for happiness, and I for endurance, and if I dare beseech thee to grant me one thing more, O thou infinite Divinity! it is that Thou wouldst cut out from my soul this love which is eating into my heart as though it were rotten wood, and keep me far from envy and jealousy when I see her happy in his arms. It is hard—very hard to drive one's own heart out into the desert in order that spring may blossom in that of another: but it is well so— and my mother would commend me and my father would say I had acted after his own heart, and in obedience to the teaching of the great men on these pedestals. Be still, be still my aching heart—there—that is right!"

Thus reflecting she went past the busts of Zeno and Chrysippus, glancing at their features distinct in the moonlight: and her eyes falling on the smooth slabs of stone with which the open space was paved, her own shadow caught her attention, black and sharply defined, and exactly resembling that of some man travelling from one town to another in his cloak and broad-brimmed hat.

"Just like a man!" she muttered to herself; and as, at the same moment, she saw a figure resembling her own, and, like herself, wearing a hat, appear near the entrance to the tombs, and fancied she recognized it as Publius, a thought, a scheme, flashed through her excited brain, which at first appalled her, but in the next instant filled her with the ecstasy which an eagle may feel when he spreads his mighty wings and soars above the dust of the earth into the pure and infinite ether. Her heart beat high, she breathed deeply and slowly, but she advanced to meet the Roman, drawn up to her full height like a queen, who goes forward to receive some equal sovereign; her hat, which she had taken off, in her left hand, and the Smith's key in her right-straight on towards the door of the Apis-tombs.

CHAPTER XXI.

The man whom Klea had seen was in fact none other than Publius. He was now at the end of a busy day, for after he had assured himself that Irene had been received by the sculptor and his wife, and welcomed as if she were their own child, he had returned to his tent to write once more a dispatch to Rome. But this he could not accomplish, for his friend Lysias paced restlessly up and down by him as he sat, and as often as he put the reed to the papyrus disturbed him with enquiries about the recluse, the sculptor, and their rescued protegee.

When, finally, the Corinthian desired to know whether he, Publius, considered Irene's eyes to be brown or blue, he had sprung up impatiently, and exclaimed indignantly:

"And supposing they were red or green, what would it matter to me!"

Lysias seemed pleased rather than vexed with this reply, and he was on the point of confessing to his friend that Irene had caused in his heart a perfect conflagration—as of a forest or a city in flames—when a master of the horse had appeared from Euergetes, to present the four splendid horses from Cyrene, which his master requested the noble Roman Publius Cornelius Scipio Nasica to accept in token of his friendship.

The two friends, who both were judges and lovers of horses, spent at least an hour in admiring the fine build and easy paces of these valuable beasts. Then came a chamberlain from the queen to invite Publius to go to her at once.

The Roman followed the messenger after a short delay in his tent, in order to take with him the gems representing the marriage of Hebe, for on his way from the sculptor's to the palace it had occurred to him that he would offer them to the queen, after he had informed her of the parentage of the two water-carriers. Publius had keen eyes, and the queen's weaknesses had not escaped him, but he had never suspected her of being capable of abetting her licentious brother in forcibly possessing himself of the innocent daughter of a noble father. He now purposed to make her a present—as in some degree a substitute for the representation his friend had projected, and which had come to nothing—of the picture which she had hoped to find pleasure in reproducing.

Cleopatra received him on her roof, a favor of which few could boast; she allowed him to sit at her feet while she reclined on her couch, and gave him to understand, by every glance of her eyes and every word she spoke, that his presence was a happiness to her, and filled her with passionate delight. Publius soon contrived to lead the conversation to the subject of the innocent parents of the water-bearers, who had been sent off to the goldmines; but Cleopatra interrupted his speech in their favor and asked him plainly, undisguisedly, and without any agitation, whether it was true that he himself desired to win the youthful Hebe. And she met his absolute denial with such persistent and repeated expressions of disbelief, assuming at last a tone of reproach, that he grew vexed and broke out into a positive declaration that he regarded lying as unmanly and disgraceful, and could endure any insult rather than a doubt of his veracity.

Such a vehement and energetic remonstrance from a man she had distinguished was a novelty to Cleopatra, and she did not take it amiss, for she might now believe—what she much wished to believe—that Publius wanted to have nothing to do with the fair Hebe, that Eulaeus had slandered her friend, and that Zoe had been in error when, after her vain expedition to the temple—from which she had then just returned—she had told her that the Roman was Irene's lover, and must at the earliest hour have betrayed to the girl herself, or to the priests in the Serapeum, what was their purpose regarding her.

In the soul of this noble youth there was nothing false—there could be nothing false! And she, who was accustomed never to hear a word from the men who surrounded her without asking herself with what aim it was spoken, and how much of it was dissimulation or downright falsehood, trusted the Roman, and was so happy in her trust that, full of gracious gaiety, she herself invited Publius to give her the recluse's petition to read. The Roman at once gave her the roll, saying that since it contained so much that was sad, much as he hoped she would make herself acquainted with it, he felt himself called upon also to give her some pleasure, though in truth but a very small one. Thus speaking he produced the gems, and she showed as much delight over this little work of art as if, instead of being a rich queen and possessed of the finest engraved gems in the world, she were some poor girl receiving her first gift of some long-desired gold ornament.

"Exquisite, splendid!" she cried again and again. "And besides, they are an imperishable memorial of you, dear friend, and of your visit to Egypt. I will have them set with the most precious stones; even diamonds will seem worthless to me compared with this gift from you. This has already decided my sentence as to Eulaeus and his unhappy victims before I read your petition. Still I will read that roll, and read it attentively, for my husband regards Eulaeus as a useful—almost an indispensable-tool, and I must give good reasons for my verdict and for the pardon. I believe in the innocence of the unfortunate Philotas, but if he had committed a hundred murders, after this present I would procure his freedom all the same."

The words vexed the Roman, and they made her who had spoken them in order to please him appear to him at that moment more in the light of a corruptible official than of a queen. He found the time hang heavy that he spent with Cleopatra, who, in spite of his reserve, gave him to understand with more and more insistence how warmly she felt towards him; but the more she talked and the more she told him, the more silent he became, and he breathed a sigh of relief when her husband at last appeared to fetch him and Cleopatra away to their mid-day meal.

At table Philometor promised to take up the cause of Philotas and his wife, both of whom he had known, and whose fate had much grieved him; still he begged his wife and the Roman not to bring Eulaeus to justice till Euergetes should have left Memphis, for, during his brother's presence, beset as he was with difficulties, he could not spare him; and if he might judge of Publius by himself he cared far more to reinstate the innocent in their rights, and to release them from their miserable lot—a lot of which he had only learned the full horrors quite recently from his tutor Agatharchides—than to drag a wretch before the judges to-morrow or the day after, who was unworthy of his anger, and who at any rate should not escape punishment.

Before the letter from Asclepiodorus—stating the mistaken hypothesis entertained by the priests of Serapis that Irene had been carried off by the king's order—could reach the palace, Publius had found an opportunity of excusing himself and quitting the royal couple. Not even Cleopatra herself could raise any objection to his distinct assurance that he must write to Rome today on matters of importance. Philometor's favor was easy to win, and as soon as he was alone with his wife he could not find words enough in praise of the noble qualities of the young man, who seemed destined in the future to be of the greatest service to him and to his interests at Rome, and whose friendly attitude towards himself was one more advantage that he owed—as he was happy to acknowledge—to the irresistible talents and grace of his wife.

When Publius had quitted the palace and hurried back to his tent, he felt like a journeyman returning from a hard day's labor, or a man acquitted from a serious charge; like one who had lost his way, and has found the right road again.

The heavy air in the arbors and alleys of the embowered gardens seemed to him easier to breathe than the cool breeze that fanned Cleopatra's raised roof. He felt the queen's presence to be at once exciting and oppressive, and in spite of all that was flattering to himself in the advances made to him by the powerful princess, it was no more gratifying to his taste than an elegantly prepared dish served on gold plate, which we are forced to partake of though poison may be hidden in it, and which when at last we taste it is sickeningly sweet.

Publius was an honest man, and it seemed to him—as to all who resemble him—that love which was forced upon him was like a decoration of honor bestowed by a hand which we do not respect, and that we would rather refuse than accept; or like praise out of all proportion to our merit, which may indeed delight a fool, but rouses the indignation rather than the gratitude of a wise man. It struck him too that Cleopatra intended to make use of him, in the first place as a toy to amuse herself, and then as a useful instrument or underling, and this so gravely incensed and discomfited the serious and sensitive young man that he would willingly have quitted Memphis and Egypt at once and without any leave- taking. However, it was not quite easy for him to get away, for all his thoughts of Cleopatra were mixed up with others of Klea, as inseparably as when we picture to ourselves the shades of night, the tender light of the calm moon rises too before our fancy.

Having saved Irene, his present desire was to restore her parents to liberty; to quit Egypt without having seen Klea once more seemed to him absolutely impossible. He endeavored once more to revive in his mind the image of her proud tall figure; he felt he must tell her that she was beautiful, a woman worthy of a king—that he was her friend and hated injustice, and was ready to sacrifice much for justice's sake and for her own in the service of her parents and herself. To-day again, before the banquet, he purposed to go to the temple, and to entreat the recluse to help him to an interview with his adopted daughter.

If only Klea could know beforehand what he had been doing for Irene and their parents she must surely let him see that her haughty eyes could look kindly on him, must offer him her hand in farewell, and then he should clasp it in both his, and press it to his breast. Then would he tell her in the warmest and most inspired words he could command how happy he was to have seen her and known her, and how painful it was to bid her farewell; perhaps she might leave her hand in his, and give him some kind word in return. One kind word—one phrase of thanks from Klea's firm but beautiful mouth—seemed to him of higher value than a kiss or an embrace from the great and wealthy Queen of Egypt.

When Publius was excited he could be altogether carried away by a sudden sweep of passion, but his imagination was neither particularly lively nor glowing. While his horses were being harnessed, and then while he was driving to the Serapeum, the tall form of the water-bearer was constantly before him; again and again he pictured himself holding her hand instead of the reins, and while he repeated to himself all he meant to say at parting, and in fancy heard her thank him with a trembling voice for his valuable help, and say that she would never forget him, he felt his eyes moisten— unused as they had been to tears for many years. He could not help recalling the day when he had taken leave of his family to go to the wars for the first time. Then it had not been his own eyes but his mother's that had sparkled through tears, and it struck him that Klea, if she could be compared to any other woman, was most like to that noble matron to whom he owed his life, and that she might stand by the side of the daughter of the great Scipio Africanus like a youthful Minerva by the side of Juno, the stately mother of the gods.

His disappointment was great when he found the door of the temple closed, and was forced to return to Memphis without having seen either Klea or the recluse.

He could try again to-morrow to accomplish what had been impossible to-day, but his wish to see the girl he loved, rose to a torturing longing, and as he sat once more in his tent to finish his second despatch to Rome the thought of Klea came again to disturb his serious work. Twenty times he started up to collect his thoughts, and as often flung away his reed as the figure of the water-bearer interposed between him and the writing under his hand; at last, out of patience with himself, he struck the table in front of him with some force, set his fists in his sides hard enough to hurt himself, and held them there for a minute, ordering himself firmly and angrily to do his duty before he thought of anything else.

His iron will won the victory; by the time it was growing dusk the despatch was written. He was in the very act of stamping the wax of the seal with the signet of his family—engraved on the sardonyx of his ring- -when one of his servants announced a black slave who desired to speak with him. Publius ordered that he should be admitted, and the negro handed him the tile on which Eulaeus had treacherously written Klea's invitation to meet her at midnight near the Apis-tombs. His enemy's crafty-looking emissary seemed to the young man as a messenger from the gods; in a transport of haste and, without the faintest shadow of a suspicion he wrote, "I will be there," on the luckless piece of clay.

Publius was anxious to give the letter to the Senate, which he had just finished, with his own hand, and privately, to the messenger who had yesterday brought him the despatch from Rome; and as he would rather have set aside an invitation to carry off a royal treasure that same night than have neglected to meet Klea, he could not in any case be a guest at the king's banquet, though Cleopatra would expect to see him there in accordance with his promise. At this juncture he was annoyed to miss his friend Lysias, for he wished to avoid offending the queen; and the

Corinthian, who at this moment was doubtless occupied in some perfectly useless manner, was as clever in inventing plausible excuses as he himself was dull in such matters. He hastily wrote a few lines to the friend who shared his tent, requesting him to inform the king that he had been prevented by urgent business from appearing among his guests that evening; then he threw on his cloak, put on his travelling-hat which shaded his face, and proceeded on foot and without any servant to the harbor, with his letter in one hand and a staff in the other.

The soldiers and civic guards which filled the courts of the palace, taking him for a messenger, did not challenge him as he walked swiftly and firmly on, and so, without being detained or recognized, he reached the inn by the harbor, where he was forced to wait an hour before the messenger came home from the gay strangers' quarter where he had gone to amuse himself. He had a great deal to talk of with this man, who was to set out next morning for Alexandria and Rome; but Publius hardly gave himself the necessary time, for he meant to start for the meeting place in the Necropolis indicated by Klea, and well-known to himself, a full hour before midnight, although he knew that be could reach his destination in a very much shorter time.

The sun seems to move too slowly to those who long and wait, and a planet would be more likely to fail in punctuality than a lover when called by love.

In order to avoid observation he did not take a chariot but a strong mule which the host of the inn lent him with pleasure; for the Roman was so full of happy excitement in the hope of meeting Klea that he had slipped a gold piece into the small, lightly-closed fingers of the innkeeper's pretty child, which lay asleep on a bench by the side of the table, besides paying double as much for the country wine he had drunk as if it had been fine Falernian and without asking for his reckoning. The host looked at him in astonishment when, finally, he sprang with a grand leap on to the back of the tall beast, without laying his hand on it; and it seemed even to Publius himself as though he had never since boyhood felt so fresh, so extravagantly happy as at this moment.

The road to the tombs from the harbor was a different one to that which led thither from the king's palace, and which Klea had taken, nor did it lead past the tavern in which she had seen the murderers. By day it was much used by pilgrims, and the Roman could not miss it even by night, for the mule he was riding knew it well. That he had learned, for in answer to his question as to what the innkeeper kept the beast for he had said that it was wanted every day to carry pilgrims arriving from Upper Egypt to the temple of Serapis and the tombs of the sacred bulls; he could therefore very decidedly refuse the host's offer to send a driver with the beast. All who saw him set out supposed that he was returning to the city and the palace.

Publius rode through the streets of the city at an easy trot, and, as the laughter of soldiers carousing in a tavern fell upon his ear, he could have joined heartily in their merriment. But when the silent desert lay around him, and the stars showed him that he would be much too early at the appointed place, he brought the mule to a slower pace, and the nearer he came to his destination the graver he grew, and the stronger his heart beat. It must be something important and pressing indeed that Klea desired to tell him in such a place and at such an hour. Or was she like a thousand other women—was he now on the way to a lover's meeting with her, who only a few days before had responded to his glance and accepted his violets?

This thought flashed once through his mind with importunate distinctness, but he dismissed it as absurd and unworthy of himself. A king would be more likely to offer to share his throne with a beggar than this girl would be to invite him to enjoy the sweet follies of love-making with her in a secret spot.

Of course she wanted above all things to acquire some certainty as to her sister's fate, perhaps too to speak to him of her parents; still, she would hardly have made up her mind to invite him if she had not learned to trust him, and this confidence filled him with pride, and at the same time with an eager longing to see her, which seemed to storm his heart with more violence with every minute that passed.

While the mule sought and found its way in the deep darkness with slow and sure steps, he gazed up at the firmament, at the play of the clouds which now covered the moon with their black masses, and now parted, floating off in white sheeny billows while the silver crescent of the moon showed between them like a swan against the dark mirror of a lake.

And all the time he thought incessantly of Klea—thinking in a dreamy way that he saw her before him, but different and taller than before, her form growing more and more before his eyes till at last it was so tall that her head touched the sky, the clouds seemed to be her veil, and the moon a brilliant diadem in her abundant dark hair. Powerfully stirred by this vision he let the bridle fall on the mule's neck, and spread open his arms to the beautiful phantom, but as he rode forwards it ever retired, and when presently the west wind blew the sand in his face, and he had to cover his eyes with his hand it vanished entirely, and did not return before he found himself at the Apis-tombs.

He had hoped to find here a soldier or a watchman to whom he could entrust the beast, but when the midnight chant of the priests of the temple of Osiris-Apis had died away not a sound was to be heard far or near; all that lay around him was as still and as motionless as though all that had ever lived there were dead. Or had some demon robbed him of his hearing? He could hear the rush of his own swift pulses in his ears- not the faintest sound besides.

Such silence is there nowhere but in the city of the dead and at night, nowhere but in the desert.

He tied the mule's bridle to a stela of granite covered with inscriptions, and went forward to the appointed place. Midnight must be past—that he saw by the position of the moon, and he was beginning to ask himself whether he should remain standing where he was or go on to meet the water-bearer when he heard first a light footstep, and then saw a tall erect figure wrapped in a long mantle advancing straight towards him along the avenue of sphinxes. Was it a man or a woman—was it she whom he expected? and if it were she, was there ever a woman who had come to meet a lover at an assignation with so measured, nay so solemn, a step? Now he recognized her face—was it the pale moonlight that made it look so bloodless and marble-white? There was something rigid in her features, and yet they had never—not even when she blushingly accepted his violets—looked to him so faultlessly beautiful, so regular and so nobly cut, so dignified, nay impressive.

For fully a minute the two stood face to face, speechless and yet quite near to each other. Then Publius broke the silence, uttering with the warmest feeling and yet with anxiety in his deep, pure voice, only one single word; and the word was her name "Klea."

The music of this single word stirred the girl's heart like a message and blessing from heaven, like the sweetest harmony of the siren's song, like the word of acquittal from a judge's lips when the verdict is life or death, and her lips were already parted to say 'Publius' in a tone no less deep and heartfelt-but, with all the force of her soul, she restrained herself, and said softly and quickly:

"You are here at a late hour, and it is well that you have come."

"You sent for me," replied the Roman.

"It was another that did that, not I," replied Klea in a slow dull tone, as if she were lifting a heavy weight, and could hardly draw her breath. "Now—follow me, for this is not the place to explain everything in."

With these words Klea went towards the locked door of the Apis-tombs, and tried, as she stood in front of it, to insert into the lock the key that Krates had given her; but the lock was still so new, and her fingers shook so much, that she could not immediately succeed. Publius meanwhile was standing close by her side, and as he tried to help her his fingers touched hers.

And when he—certainly not by mistake—laid his strong and yet trembling hand on hers, she let it stay for a moment, for she felt as if a tide of warm mist rose up in her bosom dimming her perceptions, and paralyzing her will and blurring her sight.

"Klea," he repeated, and he tried to take her left hand in his own; but she, like a person suddenly aroused to consciousness after a short dream, immediately withdrew the hand on which his was resting, put the key into the lock, opened the door, and exclaimed in a voice of almost stern command, "Go in first."

Publius obeyed and entered the spacious antechamber of the venerable cave, hewn out of the rock and now dimly lighted. A curved passage of which he could not see the end lay before him, and on both sides, to the right and left of him, opened out the chambers in which stood the sarcophagi of the deceased sacred bulls. Over each of the enormous stone coffins a lamp burnt day and night, and wherever a vault stood open their glimmer fell across the deep gloom of the cave, throwing a bright beam of light on the dusky path that led into the heart of the rock, like a carpet woven of rays of light.

What place was this that Klea had chosen to speak with him in.

But though her voice sounded firm, she herself was not cool and insensible as Orcus—which this place, which was filled with the fumes of incense and weighed upon his senses, much resembled—for he had felt her fingers tremble under his, and when he went up to her, to help her, her heart beat no less violently and rapidly than his own. Ah! the man who should succeed in touching that heart of hard, but pure and precious crystal would indeed enjoy a glorious draught of the most perfect bliss.

"This is our destination," said Klea; and then she went on in short broken sentences. "Remain where you are. Leave me this place near the door. Now, answer me first one question. My sister Irene has vanished from the temple. Did you cause her to be carried off?"

"I did," replied Publius eagerly. "She desired me to greet you from her, and to tell you how much she likes her new friends. When I shall have told you—"

"Not now" interrupted Klea excitedly. "Turn round—there where you see the lamp-light." Publius did as he was desired, and a slight shudder shook even his bold heart, for the girl's sayings and doings seemed to him not solemn merely, but mysterious like those of a prophetess. A violent crash sounded through the silent and sacred place, and loud echoes were tossed from side to side, ringing ominously throughout the grotto. Publius turned anxiously round, and his eye, seeking Klea, found her no more; then, hurrying to the door of the cave, he heard her lock it on the outside.

The water-bearer had escaped him, had flung the heavy door to, and imprisoned him; and this idea was to the Roman so degrading and unendurable that, lost to every feeling but rage, wounded pride, and the wild desire to be free, he kicked the door with all his might, and called out angrily to Klea:

"Open this door—I command you. Let me free this moment or, by all the gods—"

He did not finish his threat, for in the middle of the right-hand panel of the door a small wicket was opened through which the priests were wont to puff incense into the tomb of the sacred bulls—and twice, thrice, finally, when he still would not be pacified, a fourth time, Klea called out to him:

"Listen to me—listen to me, Publius." Publius ceased storming, and she went on:

"Do not threaten me, for you will certainly repent it when you have heard what I have to tell you. Do not interrupt me; I may tell you at once this door is opened every day before sunrise, so your imprisonment will not last long; and you must submit to it, for I shut you in to save your life—yes, your life which was in danger. Do you think my anxiety was folly? No, Publius, it is only too well founded, and if you, as a man, are strong and bold, so am I as a woman. I never was afraid of an imaginary nothing. Judge yourself whether I was not right to be afraid for you.

"King Euergetes and Eulaeus have bribed two hideous monsters to murder you. When I went to seek out Irene I overheard all, and I have seen with my own eyes the two horrible wolves who are lurking to fall upon you, and heard with these ears their scheme for doing it. I never wrote the note on the tile which was signed with my name; Eulaeus did it, and you took his bait and came out into the desert by night. In a few minutes the ruffians will have stolen up to this place to seek their victim, but they will not find you, Publius, for I have saved you—I, Klea, whom you first met with smiles—whose sister you have stolen away—the same Klea that you a minute since were ready to threaten. Now, at once, I am going into the desert, dressed like a traveller in a coat and hat, so that in the doubtful light of the moon I may easily be taken for you—going to give my weary heart as a prey to the assassins' knife."

"You are mad!" cried Publius, and he flung himself with his whole weight on the door, and kicked it with all his strength. "What you purpose is pure madness open the door, I command you! However strong the villains may be that Euergetes has bribed, I am man enough to defend myself."

"You are unarmed, Publius, and they have cords and daggers."

"Then open the door, and stay here with me till day dawns. It is not noble, it is wicked to cast away your life. Open the door at once, I entreat you, I command you!"

At any other time the words would not have failed of their effect on Klea's reasonable nature, but the fearful storm of feeling which had broken over her during the last few hours had borne away in its whirl all her composure and self-command. The one idea, the one resolution, the one desire, which wholly possessed her was to close the life that had been so full of self-sacrifice by the greatest sacrifice of all—that of life itself, and not only in order to secure Irene's happiness and to save the Roman, but because it pleased her—her father's daughter— to make a noble end; because she, the maiden, would fain show Publius what a woman might be capable of who loved him above all others; because, at this moment, death did not seem a misfortune; and her mind, overwrought by hours of terrific tension, could not free itself from the fixed idea that she would and must sacrifice herself.

She no longer thought these things—she was possessed by them; they had the mastery, and as a madman feels forced to repeat the same words again and again to himself, so no prayer, no argument at this moment would have prevailed to divert her from her purpose of giving up her young life for Publius and Irene. She contemplated this resolve with affection and pride as justifying her in looking up to herself as to some nobler creature. She turned a deaf ear to the Roman's entreaty, and said in a tone of which the softness surprised him:

"Be silent Publius, and hear me further. You too are noble, and certainly you owe me some gratitude for having saved your life."

"I owe you much, and I will pay it," cried Publius, "as long as there is breath in this body—but open the door, I beseech you, I implore you—"

"Hear me to the end, time presses; hear me out, Publius. My sister Irene went away with you. I need say nothing about her beauty, but how bright, how sweet her nature is you do not know, you cannot know, but you will find out. She, you must be told, is as poor as I am, but the child of freeborn and noble parents. Now swear to me, swear—no, do not interrupt me—

swear by the head of your father that you will never, abandon her, that you will never behave to her otherwise than as if she were the daughter of your dearest friend or of your own brother."

"I swear it and I will keep my oath—by the life of the man whose head is more sacred to me than the names of all the gods. But now I beseech you, I command you open this door, Klea—that I may not lose you—that I may tell you that my whole heart is yours, and yours alone—that I love you, love you unboundedly."

"I have your oath," cried the girl in great excitement, for she could now see a shadow moving backwards and forwards at some distance in the desert. "You have sworn by the head of your father. Never let Irene repent having gone with you, and love her always as you fancy now, in this moment, that you love me, your preserver. Remember both of you the hapless Klea who would gladly have lived for you, but who now gladly dies for you. Do not forget me, Publius, for I have never but this once opened my heart to love, but I have loved you Publius, with pain and torment, and with sweet delight—as no other woman ever yet revelled in the ecstasy of love or was consumed in its torments." She almost shouted the last words at the Roman as if she were chanting a hymn of triumph, beside herself, forgetting everything and as if intoxicated.

Why was he now silent, why had he nothing to answer, since she had confessed to him the deepest secret of her breast, and allowed him to look into the inmost sanctuary of her heart? A rush of burning words from his lips would have driven her off at once to the desert and to death; his silence held her back—it puzzled her and dropped like cool rain on the soaring flames of her pride, fell on the raging turmoil of her soul like oil on troubled water. She could not part from him thus, and her lips parted to call him once more by his name.

While she had been making confession of her love to the Roman as if it were her last will and testament, Publius felt like a man dying of thirst, who has been led to a flowing well only to be forbidden to moisten his lips with the limpid fluid. His soul was filled with passionate rage approaching to despair, and as with rolling eyes he glanced round his prison an iron crow-bar leaning against the wall met his gaze; it had been used by the workmen to lift the sarcophagus of the last deceased Apis into its right place. He seized upon this tool, as a drowning man flings himself on a floating plank: still he heard Klea's last words, and did not lose one of them, though the sweat poured from his brow as he inserted the metal lever like a wedge between the two halves of the door, just above the threshold.

All was now silent outside; perhaps the distracted girl was already hurrying towards the assassins—and the door was fearfully heavy and would not open nor yield. But he must force it—he flung himself on the earth and thrust his shoulder under the lever, pushing his whole body against the iron bar, so that it seemed to him that every joint threatened to give way and every sinew to crack; the door rose—once more he put forth the whole strength of his manly vigor, and now the seam in the wood cracked, the door flew open, and Klea, seized with terror, flew off and away—into the desert—straight towards the murderers.

Publius leaped to his feet and flung himself out of his prison; as he saw Klea escape he flew after her with, hasty leaps, and caught her in a few steps, for her mantle hindered her in running, and when she would not obey his desire that she should stand still he stood in front of her and said, not tenderly but sternly and decidedly:

"You do not go a step farther, I forbid it."

"I am going where I must go," cried the girl in great agitation. "Let me go, at once!"

"You will stay here—here with me," snarled Publius, and taking both her hands by the wrists he clasped them with his iron fingers as with handcuffs. "I am the man and you are the woman, and I will teach you who is to give orders here and who is to obey."

Anger and rage prompted these quite unpremeditated words, and as Klea—while he spoke them with quivering lips—had attempted with the exertion of all her strength, which was by no means contemptible, to wrench her hands from his grasp, he forced her—angry as he still was, but nevertheless with due regard for her womanliness—forced her by a gentle and yet irresistible pressure on her arms to bend before him, and compelled her slowly to sink down on both knees.

As soon as she was in this position, Publius let her free; she covered her eyes with her aching hands and sobbed aloud, partly from anger, and because she felt herself bitterly humiliated.

"Now, stand up," said Publius in an altered tone as he heard her weeping. "Is it then such a hard matter to submit to the will of a man who will not and cannot let you go, and whom you love, besides?" How gentle and kind the words sounded! Klea, when she heard them, raised her eyes to Publius, and as she saw him looking down on her as a supplicant her anger melted and turned to grateful emotion—she went closer to him on her knees, laid her head against him and said:

"I have always been obliged to rely upon myself, and to guide another person with loving counsel, but it must be sweeter far to be led by affection and I will always, always obey you."

"I will thank you with heart and soul henceforth from this hour!" cried Publius, lifting her up. "You were ready to sacrifice your life for me, and now mine belongs to you. I am yours and you are mine—I your husband, you my wife till our life's end!"

He laid his hands on her shoulders, and turned her face round to his; she resisted no longer, for it was sweet to her to yield her will to that of this strong man. And how happy was she, who from her childhood had taken it upon herself to be always strong, and self-reliant, to feel herself the weaker, and to be permitted to trust in a stronger arm than her own. Somewhat thus a young rose-tree might feel, which for the first time receives the support of the prop to which it is tied by the careful gardener.

Her eyes rested blissfully and yet anxiously on his, and his lips had just touched hers in a first kiss when they started apart in terror, for Klea's name was clearly shouted through the still night-air, and in the next instant a loud scream rang out close to them followed by dull cries of pain.

"The murderers!" shrieked Klea, and trembling for herself and for him she clung closely to her lover's breast. In one brief moment the self- reliant heroine—proud in her death-defying valor—had become a weak, submissive, dependent woman.

Milton Keynes UK
Ingram Content Group UK Ltd.
UKHW042227180324
439698UK00005B/516